BUZZ BUMBLE to the RESCUE

Dedicated to Matthew, Ursula, Kurt, Mike,
and *all* the preschool kids for bee-ing so inspiring;
to V.W.A. and my wonderful critique buddies;
and to the Vermont College MFA folks—
thank you all!
L.E.H.

To busy buzzy Oliver Manley bee
J.N.

No part of this publication may be reproduced,
stored in a retrieval system, or transmitted in any form
or by any means, electronic, mechanical, photocopying,
recording, or otherwise, without written permission
of the publisher. For information regarding permission,
write to Bloomsbury Children's Books USA,
175 Fifth Avenue, New York, NY 10010.

ISBN 0-439-87323-1

Text copyright © 2005 by Lynn E. Hazen.
Illustrations copyright © 2005 by Jill Newton. All rights reserved.
Published by Scholastic Inc., 557 Broadway, New York, NY 10012,
by arrangement with Bloomsbury Children's Books USA.
SCHOLASTIC and associated logos are trademarks and/or
registered trademarks of Scholastic Inc.

12 11 10 9 8 7 6 5 4 3 2 1   6 7 8 9 10 11/0

Printed in the U.S.A.   08

First Scholastic printing, May 2006

BUZZ BUMBLE to the RESCUE

by Lynn E. Hazen

illustrated by Jill Newton

SCHOLASTIC INC.

New York Toronto London Auckland Sydney
Mexico City New Delhi Hong Kong Buenos Aires

Buzz Bumble was just a medium-sized bee, but he could fly fast, dance the bee dance, and buzz and tumble with gusto.

All the bees admired his talents.

"Look at Buzz fly!"
gasped Humble Bumble.

"That Buzz sure can bring home
the nectar," said Señor Sting.

"I hope Ansel Antennae
features Buzz in the next
National Bee-Graphic,"
Ms. Bizzy said.

Ansel Antennae, the famous photographer,
was coming to the garden later that day.
Buzz's wings vibrated with joy.

Then Baby Bumble landed in the garden.
Everyone gushed over the new little bee.
"Just look at her six itty-bitty legs!" said Humble Bumble.
"Have you ever seen such a tiny stinger?" asked Señor Sting.
Ms. Bizzy cooed, "She's sweeter than all the nectar in the garden."

Baby fluttered her tiny wings.

Buzz didn't like it one bit.
Why were they droning on
and on about her?

Buzz thought they should send Baby right back to the Queen Bee.
But Ms. Bizzy told Buzz to look after Baby.
"Oh, brother," grumbled Buzz.

Buzz wanted to practice his aerobatics for Ansel Antennae's visit.
"Look out, Baby," he said. "You're in my way."

He tried to teach her to fly fast,

but she was very slow.

He showed her the first three steps of the bee dance, but Baby Bumble tripped again and again.

"The garden is a dangerous place," Buzz warned Baby. But Baby was too busy smelling the flowers to listen. Buzz showed her how to gather pollen and nectar, but Baby fell into the flowers, tumbling round and round every time.

"Wait for me," said Baby Bumble from deep inside a gladiola.

Buzz was tired of waiting for her.
"Hurry up," he said. "Ansel Antennae
is coming today!"
Baby's head appeared in the gladiola.

"Look at Baby Bumble!"
announced Humble.
"Our little fuzzy-buzzy
is covered with pollen!"

"Adorable," cooed Ms. Bizzy.

"Where's Ansel Antennae?"
asked Señor Sting. "Baby
is picture-perfect!"

Buzz was covered in pollen too, but nobody paid him any attention.
They were so busy admiring Baby, they didn't even
see Buzz performing his best aerobatics.
When Buzz flew in for a dramatic finish. . .

. . . he got bumped out and landed on his bumble bum.
"Ouch," said Buzz.

He flew to the swampy edge of the
garden and sat on a daisy all alone.
"No one cares about me anymore," he sighed.

Suddenly the garden was all abuzz. Ansel Antennae had arrived!
Buzz heard click,

click,

click,

and he turned to see Baby smiling
sweetly at the camera.

"Step back, please, Baby Bumble," said Ansel.
"The light is just right on that other leaf.
That's it, one more step back."

But as Baby stepped back,
she fell right into a Venus fly trap!

Buzz zipped over as fast as he could,
but the fly trap snapped shut.

"Help!" cried Baby.
No one knew what to do.
It was too horrible to watch.

Buzz jumped right onto the dangerous
jaws of the trap. He pried them halfway open.
"Hurry, Baby!" shouted Buzz.

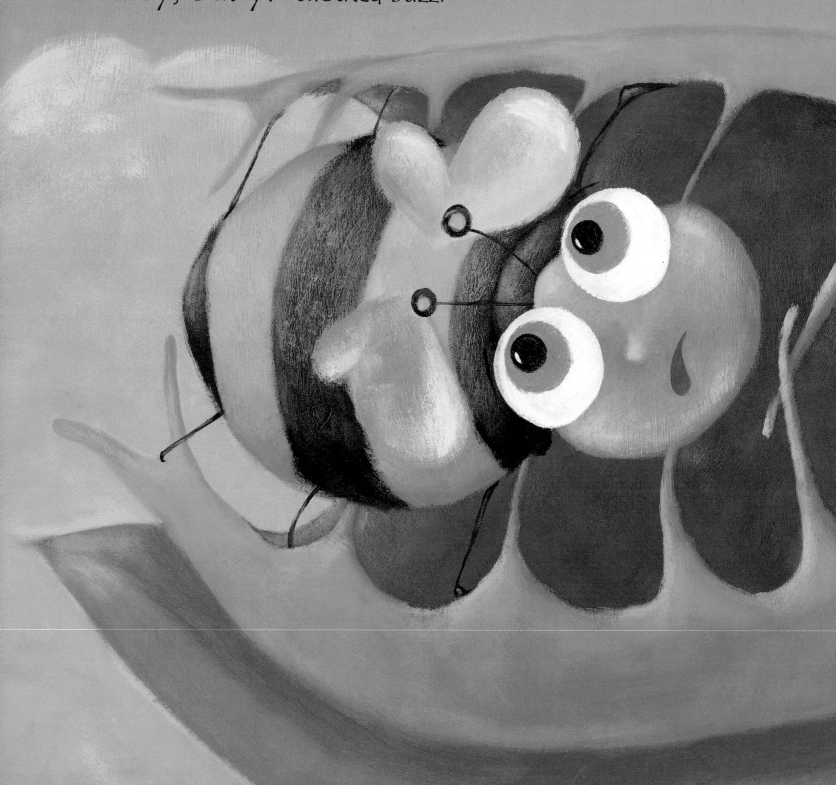

She fluttered her tiny wings.
"I can't fly out," she cried. "It's all hairy in here, and so sticky!"
"Do the bee dance," urged Buzz.
Baby began to dance, but she tripped as usual.

"That's right! Tumble toward me," Buzz said.
Daintily dancing the steps Buzz had taught her, Baby tiptoed
and tumbled toward the opening of the Venus fly trap.
"That's it!" said Buzz, holding the plant open wide.

Buzz flicked Baby out of the fly trap
with the tip of his wing.

Click, click, click went the camera.

Buzz and Baby collapsed on
a patch of sweet clover.
"You saved me, Buzz!" said Baby.
Her tiny antennae tickled his.
"Oh, brother," said Buzz.
But he tickled her back.

"Amazing!" said Señor Sting.

"Did you see Buzz's daring rescue?" asked Humble Bumble.

"That's our Buzz," cooed Ms. Bizzy.

Buzz's wings hummed with pride.

"Smile!" said Ansel Antennae. "This one's going to be perfect for the cover of the National Bee-Graphic!"

And it was.